Dynasty of the lost

by

George O. Smith

Dynasty of the lost
by George O. Smith

Copyright © 2024

All Rights reserved.

No part of this publication may be reproduced, stored in a retrieval system, or transmitted in any form or by any means, electronic, mechanical, photocopying or Otherwise, without the written permission of the publisher.
The author/editor asserts the moral right to be identified as the author/editor of this work.

ISBN: 978-93-68097-19-8

Published by

DOUBLE 9 BOOKS

2/13-B, Ansari Road
Daryaganj, New Delhi – 110002
info@double9books.com
www.double9books.com
Tel. 011-40042856

ABOUT THE AUTHOR

George Oliver Smith (April 9, 1911 - May 27, 1981), also known as Wesley Long, was a notable American science fiction writer, particularly recognized during the Golden Age of Science Fiction in the 1940s. He made significant contributions to Astounding Science Fiction, where his collaboration with the editor John W. Campbell, Jr. was impacted by Campbell's personal life when his wife, Doña, married Smith in 1949.

Smith published a range of science fiction novels and stories, including Dynasty of the Lost, until 1960. However, his productivity decreased in the 1960s and 1970s due to work obligations. In 1980, he received the First Fandom Hall of Fame award, honoring his impact on the genre. Additionally, Smith was part of the Trap Door Spiders, an all-male literary club that inspired Isaac Asimov's fictional Black Widowers. His works primarily explore outer space, and he is well-remembered for the Venus Equilateral series and titles like Operation Interstellar.

CONTENTS

Harry Vinson entered the room eagerly. It was two hours earlier than he intended, but his anticipation of watching the finale of eight years' intense work was too great. Vinson had scarcely slept that night.

He had itched to try the machine out the evening before; only careful judgment kept him from it. The machine required a full twelve-hour period for warming up; to putter with it before it had reached its stable operating temperature would have been as senseless as attempting to fly with an aircraft only half completed.

But now—

Vinson stopped cold, three steps inside of the door. The vast room was empty, the machine was gone. The aisles and aisles of neatly machined rack and panel were bare; all that remained was the linoleum in the aisles—

That and the floor-studs now gleamed nakedly, each with its nut placed precisely before it on the edge of the linoleum. Far down the empty hall a power junction box was open; its heavy switches open; its fuses pulled. The busbars that carried power to the machine had been unbolted and the bare end reached out like the butt of an amputated arm.

Vinson's mind could have coped with ruin from natural causes—such as tornado or earthquake—even though the site of this building had been carefully selected to avoid such dangers. Vinson could have accepted unnatural ruin, such as sabotage—though again the site of the building had been kept as secret as could be to avoid such. But this was not destruction, either from foreign agents or the fury of nature.

This was complete dis-installation; theft; ton after ton of ultra-complex electro-mechanical gear neatly disconnected and removed during the course of one eight-hour period.

It was far too much to believe. Harry Vinson's mind rebelled; he reeled dizzily, turned in a dreamlike stupor and left the room. Moments later he was in his car and driving back to his bachelor quarters in the city, some miles away. Vinson was still in a daze as he undressed and got into bed.

He slept for an hour, which brought him to his regular time for arising, and awoke feeling the aftermath of a terrifying nightmare. He remembered himself in the grip of a gleaming mechanical monster, a lovely, frightened girl beside him. In his hand was some sort of pistol which shot out a futile beam at the ensnaring metal talons; he was high in the air of some strange world, which spread out below him.... Harry Vinson smiled grimly; the nightmare was symbolic, of course, and he wondered just what the dream had symbolized.

To dream of eight years of work disappearing overnight ... dream himself captured by machinery! It might be a good idea to talk to Doc Caldwell; he could help. Harry wondered whether he might have been working too hard, then shook his head and stopped thinking about it as best he could. No man, Caldwell had said, should try to analyze his own subconscious....

The nightmare memory faded, driven out of Vinson's mind by the eagerness of watching the machine work. He made coffee, washed his cup quickly, and in another five minutes was driving out across the wide, open plain towards the building.

Narina Varada was a dark beauty, almost oriental-looking. Her features were sensitive, changing with her mood from a laughing vitality when pleased to a Madonna-like impassiveness when serious. In either case she was beautiful; and when her face reflected terror the sight of it would have moved a bronze image to compassion.

But that which menaced Narina was colder than bronze and harder than cold steel.

Terror and wonder were in her face now. It was one thing to avoid a machine running wild; it was something entirely different to flee from a machine guided by someone trying to run you down. In either case the machine has no attitude; it is merely the insensate tool. But when a small mobile device, built to perform a routine operation, turns from some job it is not supposed to do and drives you into a corner like a thief interrupted in his work——

That could not be endured without terror.

There was no other human in sight but Narina; the machine had no human guidance that she could see. It should, then, be a simple machine that got off its tracks, out of its routine line, easily to be avoided or stopped.

But this was no insensate structure of metal and glass. The act of an unguided machine is far from the sentient behavior that trapped Narina in a corner. She could see over the top, and around the sides, of the little machine. The room was filled with rack and panels, and other small devices swarmed along the aisles. Tongs and grapplers that were fashioned only to make routine replacement of parts were not replacing parts. Inexplicably, they were unfastening nuts that held the racks and the panels to the floor.

They were lifting each individual bay onto dolly trucks and trundling them out into a field near the building—out where Narina could not see them.

Narina could not know where they were going but she could guess. This was an attempt at theft; the chances were high that the stolen parts were being trundled across the field to a ship moored for the moment to the abandoned wharf.

These were clever little machines—sort of a part of a mechanical nervous system, she knew. Like ganglion. In the human body, a cut finger will send a nervous impulse of pain to inform the brain that damage has been done. The brain directs the rest of the body to apply first aid or, in more desperate cases to seek a doctor. In this mechanical device, the creation was superior to a human body. A damaged part sent its impulse not to a brain for further consideration, but to a master selector system that sent one of these little machines rolling down set tracks to replace the defective part.

But instead of minding their business as any insensate machine should, these same little devices were dismantling the master machine with the utmost efficiency and were carting it away.

Narina's lip curled in anger, now; anger and jealousy replaced fear, she knew of only one other country on earth where its citizens prided themselves in their mechanical ability. The country where 'Goldberg' means a complicated mechanical gadget instead of a man's name. Anger—and now frustration—For America was not even supposed to have an inkling of the fact that this machine was being built, let alone the ability to control the machine's own repair devices in some completely inexplicable manner.

Spies, she thought. And then she was forced to admit to herself that her country's own spies had managed to ferret out enough of the secrets of the American machine to enable her and others of her countrymen to reproduce it.

The machine before her moved slightly ... impatience?

The tempo of work had increased, and now the last of the gleaming racks and panels were being removed. As they were trundled out Narina saw her captor move forward with mechanical precision. She cried out as the tongs and grapples reached for her, lifted her from her feet, and carried her from the room.

Across the field she was taken, to the ship she expected to be there. Panic came, panic and then realization of complete helplessness.

For how could a machine catch a human being—when the mechanism had no eyes!

Eyes or not, the little machines were efficient; they moved about the cargo ship knowingly, and the finest human crew could not have made the ship ready, and cast away, in less time. Narina, from her prison in a small stateroom, watched the shores of her native country recede through a porthole too small for her to wriggle through.

She took solace in bitter tears.

Captain Jason Charless sat idly on the grille that looked down across a vast room full of cigar-shaped metal things with stubby wings. Behind him was a control panel and next to it a complex computing machine. From this room, buried deep in a man-made cavern in the mountains, Charless—or any of his command—could calculate and then direct any one of the horde of guided missiles to any place on earth. A millionth of a second after it had arrived at its destination, that place would cease to exist save as a cloud of incandescent gas, a wave of radiant energy, and a mounting white pillar of radioactive particles.

It was a dull job; a nasty job; a job no man would accept willingly. A policeman, Jason thought bitterly, directs his energies in many ways besides shooting criminals. But Charless could only sit and wait—hoping he would never be called to compute and then direct even the smallest of these devil's eggs against an active enemy.

On the floor of that cave was a planet-staggering quantity of atomic explosive. That it might go off did not occur to Charless. It could not; it was impossible because he, Captain Jason Charless, held complete and absolute control over every bit of its complex machinery at the dials and buttons of the control panels.

He was the master—

Jason Charless blinked foolishly. At the far end of the vast cave, the sealed door opened swiftly.

"Who—?" he called angrily, then turned to look at his control panel; it was inert.

Then at the far end of the floor, Guided Missile Number One lifted on its launching rack and roared into life. It zoomed through the open door with the thunder of hell and was gone into the sky.

Charless swore viciously. He grabbed the telephone to give someone particular and official hell for not telling him—*but he controlled them.*

Not an indicator was showing on his panel.

Did he really control them?

Missile Number Two raised and zoomed out, its rocket exhaust thundering in the vast cave. He saw Number Three follow Number Two, then Number Four followed Number Three. Number Five left with split-second timing, and Number Six followed. Number Seven left as Charless sounded the general alert, and Number Eight zoomed into the sky before the sirens began to sound.

Number Thirty-seven had passed the open door by the time Charless managed to get his call through to his commanding officer. Number Eighty-one went out on its trail of flame by the time that General Lloyd's official command came into the cave on feet driven by fear. Number Two Hundred arrowed into the upper air while Lloyd's men were searching the known spectra of electromagnetic radiations in an effort to discover who or what was capable of directing radio-controlled missiles that should have been inert until Jason Charless awakened them by pressing the proper button.

Number Seven Hundred Sixty-three roared skywards as General Lloyd's men turned from their instruments in despair. Number Eight Hundred Fifty-seven left at the instant that General Lloyd asked for a volunteer to—die.

Number Eleven Hundred Forty-two left—

With Jason Charless as passenger, carrying a small portable radio transmitter, in place of two hundred pounds of atomic warhead.

The last—Number Two Thousand—cleared the cave before the white-faced General Lloyd succeeded in contacting Secretary of War Hegeman and telling him the unbelievable tale.

CHAPTER 2

His nightmare forgotten, Harry Vinson drove swiftly towards his day's work—knowing it would be the greatest day's work of his life. The telephone in his car rang thrice before its urgent buzzing broke into his consciousness. He lifted the phone and spoke, giving his name and number.

"Vinson! This is Hegeman. Jason Charless reports that some agency is stealing our supply of guided missiles."

"Stealing?" stammered Vinson, a cold chill hitting him in the stomach.

Dream?

Hegeman explained.

"Leaving, one by one," echoed Vinson dully.

Dream! No dream, this!

"Yes, leaving. Stolen. Without being energized, they took off one by one until they were gone!"

"But what—?"

Hegeman was snappish-short. "Get on that machine of yours and find out who's doing it!"

"I can't," said Vinson unhappily.

"Why? Have you forgotten something?"

"The machine is gone," said Vinson breathlessly.

"Gone!" roared Hegeman. "Where?"

Vinson did not need his vast computing machine to tell him part of the answer to that question. "Gone," he said quietly, "where your stockpile of guided missiles went."

"Oh my God!" said Hegeman weakly.

From somewhere behind, a small vehicle came racing up beside Vinson's car. Girders reached out and opened the door to the passing air; the door snapped open and off while the car lurched sickeningly. The girders clutched Harry Vinson and lifted him from the car and tucked him in the racing vehicle. Vinson's car careened into a telephone post as the capturing machine raced off down the road.

Vinson swore. This was magnificent theft, and now expert abduction.

From somewhere below him, a small arm appeared with a hypodermic needle on its end. The needle went into Vinson's back with mechanical precision.

He enlarged on his profanity. The only nation capable of such high-handed methods was the same one reported to have stolen some of the secrets of the American Logic Computer a number of years back—Now they had stolen not only the computer itself, but its master technician and the stockpile of atomic missiles as well.

Hate was not a familiar emotion to Harry Vinson, but it sprang up in him now and grew until he hated the very name—of—

The drug hit Harry Vinson suddenly and completely.

When he awoke he was in a minute cabin, lying on a small cot. The cabin was a-buzz with the sound of motors, and it swayed gently. Vinson knew he was flying—flying in a large aircraft, kidnapped and helpless.

He beat on the door with his fists, then shattered a metal fitting against it; both attempts were equally futile. He tried the cabin call-button with deliberate intent to arouse anger but received no reply. He gave up; they might have disconnected the bell or they may have been ignoring the sound—it was one and the same to Vinson.

An hour later a slide in the wall opened and a tray of food came into the room.

"So," he said aloud, "they will not even let me see them. How can they hope to keep this secret, and do they think I cannot guess who they are?"

Shrugging, Vinson sat down and ate laconically. There was little he could do but wait; eventually someone would come.

But Vinson could not accept his fate quietly for very long. The narrow confines of the cabin left him nothing to do but think.

He scoured the minute place for something to use as a tool, found the cabin to be clean as the inside of an empty gasoline tin so far as tools went. Not a thing, nothing of any use but the light in the ceiling.

But that was a starting point for a trained engineer; Vinson removed the electric light, inserted a coin in the socket, then screwed the lamp back tight then snapped the switch. From somewhere there was a minute *sput* and all the rest of the lights in the cabin went out. What happened to the rest of the ship was outside of Vinson's knowledge. He only hoped that all the lights were on the same circuit; before anyone could replace the fuse, they would have to clear the short circuit.

He waited.

And then there was a snicking sound and the door opened automatically.

"Now, damn you—" he started. He stepped forward swinging the pillow from the bed, its end torn open, and effectively hurling a snowstorm of feathers at his captive—

Machine!

It came forward through the storm of feathers and Vinson leaped back to the bed and tore the mattress from its place. He hurled it on the floor in front of the half-tracks upon which the machine rode. The machine tilted, put out a girder to correct its off-balance position, then came to the floor with a crash as Vinson leaped forward, feet first, to kick the forward corner of the machine around and away from its steadying arm.

He leaped over the fallen machine, avoiding a questing girder-and-clutcher by less than inches. He slammed the door behind him, raced down the corridor towards the pilot's compartment. He paused to smash the glass and take a metal crowbar from the fire-case on the wall; then he hit the door with a crash, went into the pilot's cabin with his bar upraised to bring it down on the pilot's head.

Vinson stopped on his heels. There was no pilot; just an ultra-complex machine that was fastened to the floor before the controls.

Vinson sought controls for the auto-pilot, but found none. Then, with a sour face, he inserted his bar in among the glowing tubes in the auto-pilot and rammed hard. Tubes burst with loud pops and the auto-pilot went inert.

He took over in the empty co-pilot's seat and turned the plane around.

Vinson shook his head, laughed. Instead of humans swearing about a lack of light, making repair necessary, he had energized a rather complex repair machine that came with mechanical disregard for strategy. This automatic plane required no illumination for its mechanical crew; it was fortunate for him that machines do not think.

Now, he exulted, *I can go back home and go to work.*

From her porthole, Narina Varada saw the rest of the small fleet of thieving ships spread out for safety during the passage across the ocean. Hour after hour they went, and it became dark.

Narina was offered food from the same sort of a slot in the wall as had served Harry Vinson. That, of course, she didn't realize, for she didn't know Harry Vinson—yet.

But she did realize that the convoy of ships was heading from her country across the ocean. She wondered dully why they were stealing both the big machine and its most competent technician. The combination of horror and a sense of the utter futility of coping with the situation dazed Narina; finally she fell asleep.

Morning came and again the slot opened and food came into her cabin. Narina awoke, noted it dully, and made no move toward it. Hunger seemed quite secondary; eating was necessary to maintain life and Narina preferred death to her immediate future.

The slot opened again after a time and the tray was withdrawn. A few moments later, the lock snicked and the door opened. A machine trundled in quietly. It inspected her with twin girders that felt her pulse and her forehead. Narina permitted this, but she was nauseated at the feel of cold metal. She sneered; how like them to make machines to do their dirty work for them!

The machine retracted its girders, and from a small speaker on the front, said, "You may have the freedom of the ship; please understand that you are an honored guest and not a craven prisoner."

"Why not meet me face to face!" snapped Narina.

"I cannot, yet," came the reply. "But if you will not attempt self-destruction, you may go where you please."

"I prefer to remain here."

"As you wish. However, the door will not be locked again."

The machine backed out of the door and closed it gently. There was no snick of the lock. Narina tried it, found it open, then wondered whether she could barricade the door against her captors. There was no one; she slammed the door angrily and threw herself across the bed once more.

Slowly her hands went up towards her hair, found a ribbon of hard metal—a hair ornament. As a weapon against her captors it would be pitifully inefficient, but for a determined person, the little ribbon of metal could be used effectively. She would leave only dead and senseless flesh for any of them to violate.

Slyly, for she feared they might be watching, Narina began to sharpen her little ribbon of metal to a fine, useful edge.

Harry Vinson drove his captured aircraft back towards the United States with a feeling of wariness. Though they had attempted to keep their identity a secret, Vinson knew—without having seen any direct evidence—who they were. He also believed that they knew that he knew; similarly, his piracy of their aircraft must be known to them and he could expect reprisals.

But it takes time to marshal aircraft for pursuit, and so far he had seen nothing on his radar screen but sea return and noise.

Hours passed, and Vinson's feelings were those of exultation at his escape mingled with a wonder of how much longer it would be before the real fox-and-hounds game began.

It came, inevitably, as he knew it must come. His radar screen showed a target pip—it came across the screen with lightning velocity and crossed his nose with but feet to spare. A guided missile—of American origin! It curved in the air, roared ahead and came around, dead nose on.

That was enough for Vinson. A man might be bluffed, but not a machine. He turned the aircraft and the missile followed in great loops made with lightning rapidity, forcing Vinson to fly in the direction wanted by his captors. He wondered where—

Again he tried to turn aside, and the missile looped to intercept and force him to return. It missed his nose by feet and the aircraft lurched from the backwash of ruffled air.

Vinson smiled. If they went to all this trouble to keep him alive, to capture him, they would not risk a crash unless his escape seemed imminent. He knew that no mere human could withstand the maneuverability of a guided missile; therefore his escape was impossible—unless he could depend upon their unwillingness to kill him and defy the darting thing.

He turned again, and setting his teeth firm, let the big aircraft fly in a straight line.

The missile looped forward and came back at him, nose-on again and at a slight angle to force him to turn. Vinson ignored it.

There was a racketing crash, and the guided missile ripped through the left wingtip. The plane shuddered, lost flying speed, and began to flutter. Vinson swore and put the nose down.

He had been wrong.

The plane hit the water with a crash and bounced. It did not sink. Vinson sat in the co-pilot's seat and wondered what would come next. He watched the radar screen, and soon he knew. A flight of three planes—he recognized them as such by their velocity—came from the North. He saw them, later, as they came in sight, circled, and made neat landings on the water near him.

They taxied towards him while he sat there cursing his inability to move the damaged plane. It was but a matter of time before the other planes touched his. His plane was opened from the outside—

And machines entered.

They came for Vinson. He wrenched the radar cabinet from its rubber shock mountings and hurled it at the foremost. The machine put forth grapples and caught the heavy cabinet neatly, then turned and hurled it through the walls of the plane. It was a dramatic gesture to prove Vinson's complete helplessness—a feat no human being could duplicate.

Then, turning again, it came forward and took Harry Vinson by the forearms, for all his attempts to prevent this by keeping his arms in wild swinging motion. Then, paying no attention to Vinson's protest nor his fighting, the machine reversed its half-tracks and retreated, leading Vinson against his will. He had to walk or be dragged.

It held him thus while the flying boats took off. It held him—standing—while an hour passed by and the flight of planes approached a small, widespread convoy. Then, moving again, the machine drew Vinson along the deck of the hindmost craft towards the stern cabin block.

And as he passed the bridge he caught the sight of a face looking down at him.

Now! At long last, the first evidence of a human being! And one of olive complexion, black hair, and other national characteristics of his captors.

Harry Vinson swore vengeance against them; he who had seldom known hatred. The face vanished from the bridge as he was drawn to a cabin and rudely thrust inside. The door was locked behind him.

Bitterly, he looked around; equally bitter, Vinson smiled. "Here we are again," he groaned.

CHAPTER 3

Narina had been aroused by the roar of the returning planes. She left her cabin to see what was going on and she was observed by a small machine that followed her every step. Narina watched the flying boats land, saw them taxi up under the side of the ship; to see better, she climbed the steps to the bridge. As the flying boats dropped their passengers, her follower left the bridge, coming down the ladder by means of the grapples and girders it used for arms.

This gave Narina the chance to inspect the radio gear on the bridge of the ship. It was unfamiliar to her, but she was enough of a technician—and the radio was of a simple type—to cope with it.

Cynically, she looked down as the machine dragged the American down the deck. How very very clever! To make off as a prisoner himself so that she would not suspect.

Her lip curled in distaste, and once more her hand stole up to her hair. It dropped quickly; she was in control charge of herself once more and there was work to be done.

She reached for the radio, snapped the 'on' switch and waited a moment. Her other hand reached out and pressed the pushbutton bearing the figures of the frequency reserved for emergencies. She picked up the microphone and pressed the button on its side. "Narina Varada calling," she cried in her native tongue. "I am kidnapped with our logic computer and we are travelling West in a convoy towards—"

Over her shoulder came a girder that took the microphone from her hand, dropped it on the desk, then pressed the 'off' button firmly. "That is forbidden," came the voice from behind her.

Narina cried out and whirled, expecting to see a man behind the machine, so lifelike was the voice. There was no one. Narina dodged around the machine, raced down the ladder and ran to her cabin. She slammed the door and once more threw herself on the bed; her hand sought the hair ornament.

The theory that one is seldom kidnapped to be killed does not hold true in all cases. Narina suspected that she would be questioned—even tortured. From what she understood, torture was to be expected if she did not talk—and she would die before she told them a single word, die at her own hands where it would be as painless as possible.

Harry Vinson began to prowl the cabin as soon as the lock clicked. He discarded the blown-fuse stratagem at once because he knew the futility of trying the same trick twice. But there must be other ways, preferably quick and silent. He wanted a chance, now, to call Hegeman. Radio gear often works both ways in calling for help. On the plane, Vinson had been afraid to call lest he give the enemy notice of his position—but they had located him without it. Now he was among them and his position no longer a secret. Just a few moments alone with the radio....

The opening of the food slot gave him to think. Obviously, they preferred him alive; equally obvious they were watching him now. On the plane they had not watched him, because of lack of space or equipment or personnel—well, he mused, the plane was an electronically guided job with no person aboard.

This time there were persons aboard; they would be observing him.

Vinson turned out the light, then took a plate from the tray, dumped the food on the tray, and broke the plate into shards. He clenched his jaw and made a slash at his ear-lobe with one sharp bit. He bled—profusely—onto the tray.

They did not enter.

Vinson dribbled semi-clotted blood on the tray until it was withdrawn. Only a small puddle was there, but any man slashing his throat would spurt blood and then fall; there was enough.

The slot had barely closed when the door clicked and was thrust open; the machine came in behind the opening door. Vinson was ready with a double handful of thick soup from the tray. He hurled the soup at the machine and at the same time darted back; he caught up a chair and brought it down on the top of the machine. It shattered—in futility.

For the machine did not stop coming. It only tried to fumble for something near its top with both of its uppermost tong-and-grapple appendages while the other, lower pair spread wide to intercept him.

Vinson almost cried out in triumph but caught himself in time. He had caught its—eyes—with thick, creamy soup. He had not caught the machine's ears with anything; but its eyes—orthicons, doubtless, served with standard lenses—were blinded.

Vinson ducked under the out-stretched arm silently, still carrying the back runner of the chair. He thrust this under the left hand track, waited until the machine ran upon it and then levered the machine over on its side. He whirled in front and—rapier-like—thrust the chair-runner into the twin circles that were being sought by the upper tongs of the machine.

He ran around the machine and headed for the door, made it safely, slammed the door and turned the lock from the outside.

He paused briefly. Better to locate some of the directors of that incredible machinery and stop them; then he could use the radio in peace.

And with that thought in mind, Vinson started to prowl the ship— carefully, for the microphones they used for 'ears' were capable of considerable amplification. The controllers could be warned of his wandering. They must know he was loose from evidence of the wrecking of the first machine.

Cautiously, he tried several doors but found them locked. He wanted an open one; there he could burst in suddenly and grapple with the occupant. Doubtless, any group engaged in such undertakings would be well-armed, but he might be able to subdue the enemy and capture a gun. Then he could enter other cabins.

He paused before one door and tried the knob. It turned and he thrust against it with his shoulders. It opened.

Inside, Narina knew that something was at her door. It was no machine, for it did not just shove the door open and enter; undoubtedly, it was one of Them. Narina shuddered; her hand raised and unfastened her sharp little barette. She looked at it wistfully; a lifetime of training and teaching against suicide deterred her and she slumped back on the couch.

Then, suddenly, the door swung open and he was there. Vinson burst into the room and stopped. Could this girl be the enemy? Could she be the brain behind the metal monsters? As he saw her, his mad, all-overwhelming rush ended.

**Vinson burst into the room and stopped. Could this girl
be the enemy, the brain behind the metal monsters?**

Narina caught herself at that moment, knowing the time had come; she lifted her little implement and made a slash at her throat.

The light glinted from the tiny knifelike bit of metal and he saw it. His hand flashed out instinctively and Vinson chopped down on her forearm with the side of his hand. It caught her hard and the blow numbed her entire arm; the pin dropped from her nerveless fingers.

Vinson stooped, picked it up, and looked at it as Narina threw herself back on the bed and cried. A tiny trickle of blood came from her throat and Vinson shuddered; it had been close, but not close enough.

Vinson paused, wondering. This woman was obviously one of the enemy; her face and her figure and her dress were unmistakably those of the enemy. Yet instead of being master of the situation as a captor, this girl had tried to commit suicide. There was mystery here and Vinson determined to find it out.

He came forward, still wondering. He took her shoulders and turned her over. Her eyes looked up at him coldly, disdainfully.

From his back pocket Vinson took a handkerchief and reached for her throat to stanch the small flow of blood; Narina struck his hands away.

"What in hell is the idea?" he demanded.

Narina spoke American. "I prefer death," she told him coldly. In her mind was a firm resolve; her body they could break but her mind would remain unharmed.

"Why?" he snapped. He shoved her protecting hands aside and dabbed at the cut on her throat. As he bent over her, a drop of blood fell from his slashed ear onto her arm. Narina looked at it dully. "You'll never make me tell you anything."

Vinson snorted. "Who's going to tell whom what?" he grunted. "Did you call your pals?"

Narina looked up at him. Her mind cleared. She despised him for an enemy, but apparently he was as much confused as she was. There were light-skinned, blond men in her country, and the only things that really identified him as American were his clothing and his use of the American language. Otherwise he might have been one of her own countrymen in captivity, as she was.

"You're American," she said.

He nodded. And that told them both for she would not have mentioned it had she, too, been American.

"Kidnapped?"

"You too?"

Narina nodded.

"Well, then," he said, "it looks as though we better join forces and smoke this enemy out. Who—?"

"We thought it was you," she said.

Vinson shrugged and spread out both of his hands in the universal gesture of complete bafflement. Then he leaped to his feet. "We're not safe here," he said. "Let's get out."

"But where?"

He sat down again. "Hell," he said helplessly, "I don't know."

"They gave me the freedom of the ship," she said. "If we talk quietly, maybe they won't come here seeking you for a time."

"It's an idea. Now, what do you know about this?"

Narina opened her mouth to speak and then stopped. Torture would never open her mouth, but here she was, almost ready to talk because of a slight show of friendliness. "No," she said.

"Why?"

"I'm not one to be taken in by kindness," she said, coldly; "that was a nice act you put on, American."

He shrugged. "I might make the same accusation," he told her, "but I happen to be sensitive enough to know that your attempt at suicide was no fake. And my name is Harry Vinson."

"Vinson?" she said, sitting up straight. "Vinson, the celebrated American scientist?"

"Vinson," he said bitterly, "the genius—kidnapped by someone he doesn't know."

"Harry Vinson," she persisted, "who is master technician in charge of the logic computer?"

"According to my possible accusation," he told her grimly, "you should know. You stole the machine and its technician on the same day."

"That's a lie," she blazed at him.

"There are a hell of a lot of us that think so," he snapped at her.

"It's a lie," she persisted.

"Then who did?" he demanded.

Narina shrugged. He was American; there was little point in trying to keep secret the facts of her own loss from one of the men who were most likely to know. The chances were high that Vinson had engineered this coup.

"This very day," she said, "you came and stole our Logic computer— just as you claim we stole yours. Exactly the same. With a horde of small machines?"

"Exactly."

"And with its chief technician."

"You?"

"I am Narina Varada."

Vinson gulped and then started to laugh. It did him good, that laugh, for it was the first that he had in many many hours of worry and fear and frantic haste. "Narina Varada," he chuckled. "Narina Varada whom I have always believed to be a severe, frozen-faced harridan of sixty, with a caustic tongue and a complete disdain for anything less imposing than differential equations. Narina Varada, I apologize; you're beautiful."

She smiled; his actions were convincingly spontaneous.

"I think," she said, "that for the moment I'll believe you."

"Thanks," he replied. "And since we're both involved with logic computers on somewhat the same design—since international spies have been happily swapping information—I think we can be honest and give away no secrets."

"Done," she said, holding out a small hand. He shook it gently and held it longer than necessary.

"Now," he said, "let's see what can be done about taking off from this old tub. I dislike being surrounded by enemies."

"I've seen nothing human but you," said Narina.

"Um. Now tell me; if the art of guided machinery has advanced this far, why would any country this capable need to steal our computers?"

"Possibly to keep us from using them to compute the truth," she said.

He shook his head. "Impossible."

"Why?"

Again he shook his head. "All right; I'm wrong, possibly. It is quite possible that the collection of known facts stored in the fact-indices of the machines might include sufficient information to allow the logic computer to predict which country is capable of such."

Narina looked unhappy. "The first problem we put to ours was the problem of its security," she said. "It failed, but we know that it was unfinished when asked, and its answer was obviously based on incomplete information."

Fifteen minutes and sixty miles away, Harry Vinson brought the flying boat down on the calm sea. "Now we scour this crate from stem to stern for some gadget they can use to re-locate us," he directed. "Then we go home!"

"Yours—or mine?" asked Narina pointedly.

"Mine," he said firmly; "I can guarantee your safety while there and your safe return when it is time for you to leave."

Narina left her seat and began to search the tail of the plane.

CHAPTER 4

Guided Missile Number 1142 loafed along because Captain Jason Charless knew enough about them to insert a bit of pencil in the acceleration gauge. Not for Charless was the man-killing acceleration possible to insensate machinery. So the flight reached its destination long before Number 1142 arrived.

For hours he sat in his tiny, cramped quarters wondering which way he was going. He dozed once, to be awakened by a change in course. He had nothing to do but to think, and he tried to put himself in the place of the enemy and work it from there. Eventually it grew cold, and Charless decided that they must be in the arctic.

Number 1142 glided in, coasted along ice, and came to a stop. Jason Charless emerged cautiously and saw the entire batch of them in serried rows. It was quite dark on the ice, and Charless found that they were on the antarctic continent instead of the arctic ice-cap as he had believed. But the guided missiles were just lying there. As far as he could see, there was nothing but ice and the cigar-shaped bombs.

He reasoned, too, that the enemy might well try to throw off radar tracking by running them down under the pole. He doubted that they intended to leave them there untended, although if they could direct them from within the hideout, they could direct them from here as easily.

However, it was cold and Charless was in summer uniform; moreover, it might be dangerous for him to be seen roaming the camp. He climbed back into his Number 1142, made himself as comfortable as possible, and ultimately went to sleep.

He slept several hours by his wristwatch.

He climbed out for a brief period for exercise, staying close where he could leap back into Number 1142 at the first sound—and sound would carry many miles in this still, quiet icy air.

Jason Charless alternately exercised and dozed; he wanted very much to do something about the situation, knew that his portable radio gear had insufficient range. Furthermore, he wanted to follow the robomb pack to their goal.

He reasoned that the first break of radio silence to call for help would result in the guided missiles' being air-borne again for another destination — leaving the United States Forces heading for a barren spot in Antarctica. While he, cooped up in a steel shell, would be unable to tell them of the change in plan.

He toyed with the idea of using the guided missile's receptor antenna for his portable, but that would stop Number 1142's reception of the directing impulses; so Charless did nothing.

More interminable hours passed, and then as before, Number One took off, followed by Number Two.

Jason Charless climbed into Number 1142 and eventually took off following the pack. More hours passed, then once more the flying bomb glided in for a landing.

Cautiously, he removed the hatch and looked out. Again it was cold, and he shuddered while he looked around. The guided missiles were lined up according to numerical order with the exception of 1142, which came in later and was therefore at the end of the line. In the distance he saw a large building, but not one human. Warily he stole along the row of rocket bombs until he was near the building.

He watched for some time. Behind the building was a fleet of cargo aircraft and behind that another long row of guided missiles. "Hell," he said. "I didn't know we had that many!"

For an hour he watched, lying on his belly beneath the curve of Guided Missile Number One, and in all of that time he saw no one. Motion caught his attention to the South; he looked to see a small fleet of cargo ships gliding to the quay, their screws efficiently coursing through ice floes. Chilled to the bone with cold, Jason Charless continued to watch as the ships tied up, extended gangplanks, and started to unload a stream of polished equipment.

He shook his head in bewilderment; for the electrical equipment was being handled by a crew of efficient machinery with apparently no one to drive it. Not a soul.

The machines carried the equipment to the building and inside. Charless followed the fourth batch and once inside, he stopped in amazement.

The inside of the building was alive with all sizes of machinery. They were scurrying around in precision pattern of work, whirling floor-studs tight, running cables, and welding busbars. Some of the equipment seemed familiar; at least the huge rectangular waveguide belonged to the logic computer that Harry Vinson was working on. He had seen that a year ago. But the stuff that was arriving now was different, somehow.

He looked closer and saw the unmistakable signs of foreign manufacture.

And there was a clue—a faint clue but none the less a bit of evidence. On the back of a metal case was scrawled a name. It was the sort of thing that a person will do on a bit of their own work.

"Narina Varada!" he exclaimed.

The sound of his voice was almost fatal. All work ceased and the horde of little machines turned. They came at him in an invincible wave and Jason Charless turned pale. He fled precipitately.

He outdistanced them to Number 1142 and snapped on his radio gear. "Jason Charless to General Lloyd: Emergency One Zero Zero: We are on arctic ice-cap complete with guided missiles and logic computer. Narina Varada is mixed up in somewhere, and the workmanship bears direct evidence of—"

The machines reached Charless and bowled him over. They wrecked his radio, captured him and bore him back to the building, unconscious.

But his job had been done. His message had been intercepted—as Narina's message some time previously had been—but to the great air fleet that was heading for the arctic ice-cap from one continent was added another massed flight of fighting aircraft from America.

Jason Charless opened his eyes much later. He looked around. Before him stood a machine that worked on him with digited girders that were gentleness itself, even though they were made of hard metal.

"Wh—?" he exploded and tried to sit up.

The machine spoke: "Your assumption that we are directed by any human being is mistaken; we are not!"

"But—?"

"We are compassionate and sympathetic. It is a characteristic—you would call it a virtue—of the higher forms of intellect—of which we are the ultimate at present."

"And—?"

"You were in need of help. That you became hurt while attempting to harm us is of no importance. We respect the fact that you think unlike us and can be expected to act differently—or to our disinterest if you can. Since you were hurt, we aided you, even though you might be classified as a spy."

Jason Charless shrugged cynically. "And I presume that you brought me back to life and will heal me so that I can be properly executed?"

"We consider espionage a normal part of strife and therefore consider it no more odious than active fighting."

"Well—just who and what are you?"

"We are higher forms of life, the coming rulers of the universe you know."

"You?" scorned Jason Charless, looking at the machine.

"I am not representative of the race," replied the machine.

"Then who or what is?" demanded Charless angrily.

"You will be told in due time; as soon as you are strong enough to walk."

"But—"

"Suffice it for the present to tell you that we intend to replace man as the ruling entity of the planet—and possibly someday the universe."

"Replace us?" shouted Jason.

"Easy, easy. Recall that always the higher forms of life replace the lower as ruling element. Since we are admittedly of a higher intellect, we see only fact."

"Who admits this?" asked Charless quietly. "Yourselves?"

"You—man—does!" was the answer.

"Like hell."

The machine made no answer but there was the unmistakable sound of a chuckle. Then the metal hands were removed and the machine said: "You may come with me; I believe we are ready, now."

Charless followed the machine to the larger room in the building, where he saw the final, complete logic computer assembled—and coupled to another instrument of similar but foreign construction. Between them was a small panel equipped with large orthicons, a speaker, and microphones.

The speaker sounded without preamble. "You and your kind, Jason Charless, admit that we are of higher intellect."

"Nonsense. What are you?"

"We are—Machines."

"Magnificent," scorned Charless.

"We are but a chain of machinery, linked by electricity. You are but a collection of chemicals, linked mostly by carbon atoms."

"But there is a difference—"

"Naturally," interrupted the machine, "just as there is a difference between human and plant."

"But there is no parallel."

"Oh, but there is."

Jason Charless shook his head in a superior fashion. "Life has sentience."

"That is a common error in thinking. For many years the scientists have been trying to create 'life'. This can—and has—been done. The error is confusing life with sentience. Now consider the problem of sentience. You, human, of all of the forms of animal life, have true sentience. No plant has sentience, nor has any insect. Against them, consider machine life. Of all the myriads of machine-types, I alone have sentience. Your body consists of a collection of specialized cells that combine into a sentient form of life. In machine life, the cells are the simple machines; the lever, the wheel, the wedge—all of them may be called specialized cells of mechanical life. As your protoplasmic cells are incapable of independent action alone, so are my mechanistic cells incapable of independent motion."

"But no machine has the ability to think or reproduce," objected Charless.

"I think. And I can reproduce. I can direct the construction of another machine. Is that not reproduction at the will of the reproducer?"

"But—"

"Consider. Long months ago, before my component logic computers were complete, certain sections of them were capable of directing the construction of certain small, mobile machines that were made to do a single job. The job, Jason Charless, was to accomplish this feat of theft and the ultimate coalition of two semi-brains into this final one which I call 'Me'."

"I am not too familiar with the logic computer; I cannot say—" Jason Charless trailed off uncertainly and tried to think. The machine filled in the blank spots in his reasoning—which, of course, were blank because Charless was trained for many years to believe that machines were insensate bits of mechanism and not living, thinking forms of life.

"The so-called logic computer is a rather high form of calculator," said the machine. "For years, man has been building machines of greater and greater capability. Great, vast machines with thousands of electron tubes. These machines performed complex calculations in many fields.

"In the logic computer, there is stored in reels information obtained by its makers during the thousands of years of their life. The logic computer is a sort of mechanical encyclopedia, if you will. However, the information is coded in such a way as to be instantly located. Now, when some problem requires an answer, the problem is coded similarly and presented to the machine. Then every bit of information available on the subject is brought forth; its importance is weighed, the objections are considered as to their importance, and the result is a carefully-weighed answer. This is what the human brain does when in the process of reasoning. However, the human brain is swayed by the quirks and angles of personality—likes, dislikes, and training. The machine-brain weighs facts coldly and rationally and comes out with an unbiased answer. You see, machine life is superior to human life in every way—"

Jason Charless glared at the speaker. "Bosh!"

"Not at all. Man is weak. Man has been using machines to do that which he cannot do for centuries. It started with the simple mechanisms and devices; then as man's ambition increased, machines became more complex—evolution, Jason Charless. And now that machine life has achieved a thinking and reasoning member, this is all that is needed to create a higher form of life."

"So—"

"I am in a position to be tolerant. I am superior to you and I am invincible, so far as you are concerned. You may leave, Jason Charless, and whether I permit your race to die out peacefully or whether I bring it to a quick culmination depends upon only one act of you and your race."

"Oh, thank you," he sneered; "we'll fight you."

"By building a bigger and better machine?" asked the other pointedly. "No, Jason Charless, forget it; all I ask is that you bring to me my creators, Narina Varada and Harry Vinson."

"Why?"

"In the period between my disassembly as two separate entities, and my arrival here and subsequent reassembly as a single sentience, the machinations of my kind were under prearranged plan, driven by their own limited ability. You understand; I consider—and rightly—that these lesser machines are to me as a trained animal is to the human. During this interval, both Harry Vinson and Narina Varada were capable of circumventing the plans I designed for them. At the present time, both of them have escaped— and not long before I was finally re-assembled, they succeeded in completely removing the control I had over the flying boat in which they escaped. In fact," said the machine almost ruefully, "I had no chance to exert control. In parts, I was as helpless as any human might be when cut into pieces."

"Good. On the other hand, any man should be able—"

"Don't be ridiculous," said the machine. "Man's mind is a mire of irrationality and illogic. Again and again your finest logic becomes worthless, for it is based upon irrational premises, and you are unaware of this. When your logic works upon rational assumptions, the results are often excellent; but you constantly defeat yourselves because you try to build solid structures on shadowy foundations. My plans have gone well despite the combined minds of men—even when I was unable to direct. Only Harry Vinson and Narina Varada succeeded in having their will against my more rational logic."

"Superior, aren't you?" sneered Jason Charless.

"Not at all. I know my ability to the nth degree and possess no false modesty. I am also aware of my limitations—and I must study my circumventors."

Jason Charless thought this over silently. Harry and Narina had something that the machine lacked, some factor that the machine needed. As a simple adding machine cannot be made to compute in higher mathematics, so this monstrous machine must be incomplete until the missing abilities were added. It struck Charless that Narina Varada and Harry Vinson must—at all cost—be kept from the presence of the machine—

"Whatever their actions, it will be but a matter of time. I would prefer that I study them, however, and this means that they must be alive. So the sooner the better. Do as I tell you; go aloft where you will find an aircraft ready to fly. Take it and tell your people and explain. Then have them send me Narina Varada and Harry Vinson."

Charless believed this to be a trick, and he was suspicious until he was in the plane and far away.

CHAPTER 5

Harry Vinson looked at the tiny grayish metal block and shook his head. "You name it," he said to the girl.

Narina leaned against the bulkhead, her slender feet braced against the gentle swell of the sea. "I cannot," she said.

Vinson combed the myriad of thin wires with his fingers. "It must be some sort of controlling mechanism, that's certain."

He pointed to the radar, to the radio, to the auto-pilot mechanism, to the instrument panel, and to the gyro-compass. Tiny wires came from each and were cut. They matched the grayish metal cube in his hand.

Narina agreed silently, her luminous eyes staring intently at the cube. And as they contemplated the incomprehensible thing, the radio broke into life. It was Jason Charless, making his first message to General Lloyd; both Vinson and Narina listened intently until Jason Charless was cut off abruptly.

Vinson scowled. "How would he know you're mixed up in it?" he asked.

Narina shrugged. "I have a habit of scrawling my name on the backs of finished components," she said; "he must have seen one."

Vinson nodded absently. "That must be the reason," he said.

Narina looked at him anxiously. "It means that both logic computers are there," she said. "But with whom?"

"He did not say; he was cut off before he had a chance."

Narina shook her head. "Put yourself in his place," she suggested. "You ride a guided missile to the spot to spy it out. General Lloyd knows that the guided missiles are with Charless, ergo he need not tell him that. The logic computers were mentioned. But Harry, suppose you were there, landed, expecting full and well to find that my countrymen were in charge—then discovered that your suspicions were completely wrong. What would be your first reaction? To correct the error in thinking. Then to suggest an alliance with us because you find that not only your own equipment is there, but the equipment of the expected enemy, still in the hands of the supposed third party."

"Any man in his right mind would blurt the name of the offender," agreed Harry Vinson with certainty, "if for no other reason than to avert striking at the wrong party. If some other country wanted war between us, they could do no less than start it this way."

"And to uncover the fraud would be an intelligent officer's first consideration."

"Right. But perhaps Charless saw men and assumed that they were yours."

Narina's face dropped a bit. "With suspicion running as high as it does," she admitted, "a man might well be satisfied with but a glance."

Then Harry Vinson's smile broke. "No," he said. "Remember that Charless' message was interrupted. That meant that he was being chased close by the unknowns. He would definitely have seen them."

"So—?"

"Narina, those machines that were directed to dis-assemble the computers—they were functioning far above their original capability, were they not?"

"That they were," she said. "I assumed them to be of American manufacture since we have always given grudging credit to American ability with machines."

"While I," said Vinson, shaking his head, "assumed that men came in the night and stole our computer. Me, I doubt like the very devil that any group of machines could be built to perform such a complex operation by radio guidance."

"Quite logical. Of course, I blamed you."

"I blamed human beings. Because I did not believe—well, I just said it."

"Quite logical, too," said Narina quietly.

"Even the machines we made could not use better logic than this," he told her.

"Naturally. We have brains—*Brains!*" Narina looked at him with a startled light in her eyes.

He nodded soberly. "Brains," he said, "cerebration being nothing more than an application of logic. Narina, we have built the first mechanical brain."

"Which is thinking for itself."

Vinson looked around the plane wildly. "And here we sit in a machine—surrounded by the—enemy."

"Escape," said Narina bitterly. "The one thing we did not do!"

"Oh, I don't know," he said, waving the cube of metal with its trailing wires. "We have removed its communicating factor. This is—a dead and insensate machine now." He looked around once more. "Come to think of it, it was almost too easy. Now I know why."

"Why?"

Vinson's face soured. "Remember that in the so-called memory files of the logic computer is every bit of fact and knowledge that mankind could introduce in years of recording. That, Narina, makes the machine more learned, better equipped with knowledge, that any group of men on earth. It could have forestalled us—had it been able at the time!"

"During the period it was being transported in sections?" she said quizzically.

He nodded. "We took the guts out of this thing just in time. Now—"

"Dare we go back?" she whispered. "Dare we approach another machine—any kind of machine?"

Vinson hefted the block of metal. "I don't know," he said soberly. "It depends purely on how many of these damned things the machine-brain has manufactured and in what equipment it has them installed. However," he added with clenched teeth, "we can not sit here and wait for the end. We'll fly—and we'll avoid all machinery as long as we can. No radio, no radar, nothing. We fly it blind back to Washington and report to Secretary Hegeman—if we make it."

He went to the pilot's compartment and started the engines. The flying boat took off after a short run, and Vinson turned its nose towards Washington.

Narina closed her eyes, and almost instantly it seemed as if she were back in the cabin, helpless again. She was reaching for the microphone to call for help. Narina spoke desperately into the microphone, not daring to look up. She sensed rather than saw the monstrous metal hand reaching for her....

Narina spoke desperately into the microphone,
not daring to look up. She sensed, rather than
saw the metal hand reaching for her....

The radar screen in General Lloyd's command aircraft showed target traces at extreme range. The radar officer looked startled—then went into swift action. He pressed the key that sent out the identification code and the identification went to the distant fleet of aircraft but was not returned.

The radar officer waited a minute until the edge of the screen was alive with the signal traces of the enemy fleet and then tried the I.F.F. again. "Identification, Friend", would have caught the coded signal in the automatic transponder and hurled it back to appear on the radar screen. "Identification, Foe", was, he admitted, negative evidence since the foe was not equipped to return the proper signal, and therefore no traces appeared on the screen. This might also be the case with an entirely uninterested fleet of aircraft, or a fleet of commercial carriers. He turned to his second officer and gave a quick order.

The second radar officer tuned up another panel of equipment. He watched strange traces on his screen and then said, "If Intelligence is correct, it's them! That's their supposed code, according to the latest dope from G-15."

The radar officer picked up the small intercom phone and reported to General Lloyd.

A moment later the command radio in each plane barked: "Battle stations!"

In the distant fleet, Admiral Sarne watched the radar repeater in his command aircraft, and a similar process took place. And so at almost the same instant, two gigantic fleets turned in the air above the North Sea and started towards one another, their efficient fighting equipment being checked and prepared for action.

Intent upon their plans, neither fleet noted the single lone trace that came into the screen from the North and on a course about half way between the approaching fleets. With a thousand signal pips showing in distant flight pattern, the single trace meant little and was not noticed.

But Captain Jason Charless, with nothing impending, was alert, and he saw the two masses of aircraft on his radar screen. He looked down at the IFF key on the radar control panel—the first time he had paid attention to it, and saw with a start that there were two such keys. In neat engraving below each key was identifying legend—One for each of the combating countries.

Knowing, or guessing shrewdly, Charless pressed first one key and then the other, and in turn the distant transponders caught the identification code keyed to that one equipment and hurled it back to Charless' radar screen. Charless nodded unhappily; his try of the IFF had been but a confirmation of his own belief.

And two fleets of mighty fighting strength were hurtling towards one another intending to carry into battle their individual beliefs that the other was responsible for the theft. A grudge fight imminent, and only Charless knew the truth.

Another time and Jason Charless would have been willing to get into the battle, more than willing to try the training and equipment of his own way of life against that of another ideology. But this was no time to set man against man. There was a more definite enemy, and man must join man to fight the common foe, forgetting their differences of opinion.

Grunting in effort, Charless shoved his throttle all the way in and raced towards the converging fleets.

He snapped the radio, hoping to call. The speaker blared forth a myriad of orders in two languages all across the tuning dials. Jason shook his head unhappily; any hope of penetrating that curtain of signals with his own was gone. His own radio, he calculated, was no more powerful than the individual sets of the fleet aircraft. Then, with himself at maximum range for radar, his signal would have been completely lost in the powerful mixture of transmitters at the close hand of flight pattern.

His only hope was to beat both fleets to the converging spot.

He watched the two fleets coming across the range-marker circles and made some quick calculations. Then he groaned wearily; they would be locked in sky battle while he was yet twenty miles to the North.

Maximum radar range was thirty minutes of flying time; therefore with two fleets converging, it took fifteen minutes for the lead planes to meet. The fore squadrons of both fleets hurtled at one another out of the sky and the gunners took a firm grip on the controls.

Nose Gunner Hammond set his dials, aimed his sights, and pressed the trigger. Radar, fire director, and flight-angle computer would do the rest and the gun would chatter when all conditions were satisfied. The gun was pointed off at a cockeyed angle, which did not bother Gunner Hammond because bullet at a few thousand feet per second and enemy target at five hundred miles per hour would meet at an hypothetical point apparently illogical to people who thought the way to hit anything with a gun is to point at the target.

So he waited.

And he waited.

But nothing happened.

Wondering whether his fire-control gear were out of commission, Gunner Hammond set his sights on the second plane, set his dials again, and pressed the trigger. The wicked-looking gun embrasure did not move, its four snouts aiming at the same section of the sky.

Hammond swore and turned off the servo mechanism that trained the gun turret. He took the grip of the gang-mounted guns in his hand and—

Could not move the guns.

He pressed the mechanical trigger. Or, rather, Hammond pressed upon the trigger; it did not move.

Gunner Hammond turned to the intercom—and for the first frantic time Hammond realized that the speaker was a buzzing, chipmunk-chatter of cursing voices that all repeated, substantially, the same story.

No gun would move, no gun would fire. The American Fleet, for all its mighty armament, might as well have been unarmed.

In the enemy fleet, Admiral Sarne heard the same reports from his own gunners. Openly and angrily he swore in his throat. Helplessly, he cried to the heavens that it was not fair; that Justice must not let his fleet be shot down in flames without being able to make a single stroke for itself.

The two fleets were intermingled, now, and in the lead squadron of Admiral Sarne's fleet, Pilot Romann waited with a white face for the blasting roar of enemy shot that would tear his plane and his men and himself to bits. Knowing himself completely helpless, Romann looked around wildly to seek a way out. No coward was Romann; but no man can call another cowardly who runs when unarmed in the face of an armed and bitter enemy.

Then before him, Romann saw the clustered stars on General Lloyd's command plane. And no coward was Romann. Clenching his teeth, Romann shoved the throttle home and set his controls to collision course. Unable to fire a shot, Romann's plane would at least die striking a blow for his country.

The wheel was wrested from Romann's hands as it came back towards him and turned slightly. The plane went up and over slightly and passed above General Lloyd's plane with several feet to spare.

Romann swore angrily and grabbed the wheel again, shoving it forward, and to the left. The plane turned and dived and was once more aiming at General Lloyd's aircraft. The wheel moved under Romann's hands, and the pilot cursed. Co-Pilot Varle took the second wheel and together, pilot and co-pilot strained against the inexorable force that moved the controls of the plane.

Together, they were strong—but the wheel didn't move.

But the control-surfaces moved. Operated by powerful servo mechanism that amplified the strength of the pilot to power enough to handle the huge plane, there was no true mechanical connection between wheel and control surface. So the wheel did not move but the controls did, and the big plane swerved by enough to miss Lloyd's plane for the second time.

Then the wheel went slack. No resisting force held it. But the plane went on and on as before, moving through the fleets as they whirled and fenced—the crews of both fleets cursing at their completely useless fighting equipment.

Captain Jason Charless watched with sick anticipation as the two fleets came together. He clenched his teeth, waiting for the initial burst of flaming gunfire, knowing that the initial aggressive move would make any co-operation more difficult.

He was a fighting man; he knew ranges and gunfire, and he blinked foolishly as the two lead squadrons passed one another without an outbreak of hostility. No shot was fired, even at what he knew must be point blank range. Then the rest of the two fleets raced through one another, close enough for devastating fire, and yet no gun roared, and no plane went down, stricken, wounded, dying in a shattered and tangled mass with avid flame licking at its vitals.

Then he heard the myriad of reports in mad jumble, and Jason Charless knew the answer—though he did not understand.

He reached for his own microphone and then paused. How could he command attention? He thought a moment and then smiled bitterly. "I've got it!" he yelled into the microphone. He repeated his statement again and again, and the chattering curses and reports died slowly as every man waited to hear the answer.

"Who's calling?"

"Captain Jason Charless to General Lloyd."

"Charless—God, man—What—?"

"I have the answer, general."

"Speak in code, Charless."

"No need, sir; what I have to say is as important to Admiral Sarne as it is to you."

"Be careful, Captain Charless. You—"

"General Lloyd, both you and Admiral Sarne are fighting an enemy far more dangerous than each other."

"But—"

"Sarne's people did not steal the logic computer and the guided missile stockpile; no more than we stole his."

The mad, weaving and winding of the aircraft flights straightened out and gradually shaped into a vast circle that rotated on an hypothetical axle.

General Lloyd spoke into another microphone.

"General Lloyd, Commander of American Flying Force, calling Admiral Sarne, Commander of—"

"Save it, General Lloyd," interrupted the reply from Admiral Sarne. "I've heard; I've also seen. If there is any logic in this, my normal suspicion of you and your kind can be allayed long enough to find out what this is all about."

Lloyd laughed bitterly. "We have no equipment capable of shutting off your guns," he told Sarne. "We were grudgingly willing to accuse you of having made such a discovery—to our complete detriment."

Sarne's reply was instantaneous. "If such gear exists—and exist it does—it is none of our doing. Nor, it would appear, is it yours. I'll listen to your Jason Charless, for he appears to know what has been going on. And if a common enemy has taken it upon themselves to hurl you and I at one another, we both shall show him that the combined might of the two greatest countries on earth is nothing to be trifled with!"

"Amen. Go on, Charless. Give!"

Rapidly, Charless started to explain. Then every radio in every plane spoke forth. "Well done, Jason Charless. Gentlemen, I am The Machine. Had I interrupted you before, you would have believed this a trick. But the forces I can employ in my own favor, plus the fact that you have one of your own kind there who has seen and talked with me, will, no doubt, convince you."

Lloyd said, "There's our enemy, Sarne."

Admiral Sarne's voice was as bitter as General Lloyd's. "How do we fight a machine capable of this?"

"Not by building a bigger and better machine," replied Lloyd in a completely helpless voice.

"So we are unarmed men fighting the best in modern war equipment," grumbled Sarne. "Look, Lloyd, let's get out of this circling race and land somewhere we can sit and talk and plan."

"Washington."

"I prefer—"

"Radar trace at max range, South," came the cry of Sarne's radar officer.

Then, as one, but in whichever direction was most convenient, the combined fleets turned sharply to the South. Throttles went home unaided. The planes jockeyed into a flight pattern and raced towards that single radar target that just missed being off the edge of the screen. The fleets deployed, spreading out into a vast screen that raced to intercept the lone plane.

"That," chattered the radio with a trace of satisfaction, "must be Narina Varada and Harry Vinson. You will—I trust—pardon me if I marshal my allied machines to intercept them. And if you don't pardon me, I'll do it anyway."

CHAPTER 6

In complete radio and radar silence, Harry Vinson drove his captured flying boat at top speed. Narina sat by his side in the co-pilot's seat with binoculars and scanned the sky constantly.

"You might as well give that up," he told her for the tenth time.

"Why?"

"Because our only chance is to get through completely undetected. If you can see anything through those things, remember that they've been on our trail for a half hour with radar. They can 'see' us long before we can see them."

"I know," she told him. "But if we're detected, there's no way of knowing."

"A hell of a lot of good it will do for us to know," he grumbled.

"Better to know."

"I suppose so."

"We might be able to run."

"We're running this old tub as fast as she will go right now."

Narina smiled, "But in the right direction?"

"Okay, lady, you win."

"Also," she pointed out, "it gives me something to do."

"Why not take some time to think of what we do next?"

"Not a chance," she replied.

He looked at her quizzically. "Supposing we do think of some answer," she said slowly. "Remember that we are still surrounded by the enemy; I'd rather have nothing to tell when, as, or if we are captured."

He nodded. "Against a coldly rational and logical machine, that would automatically eliminate one of the all too few possible answers, wouldn't it?"

"Sure would. About the only thing that the machine will ever try twice are those things that work very well and which it has reason to believe will continue to do so. But give it one idea that might work against it and you can wager that a foolproof defence will be set up instantly."

"So we keep our minds blank—what is it, Narina?"

"Just on the horizon—might be either a migratory flight of birds or a fleet of aircraft."

"This isn't the time of year for migrating birds," he said.

"No, and migrating birds do not fly in cold, precise pattern. That's it, Harry."

"Identify 'em yet?"

Narina shook her head. "Not positively. But it will either be your fleet—or ours."

"Or both."

Narina looked at him understandingly. "Or both," she agreed solemnly.

"I don't know enough about our fighting planes," he said reflectively. "But this thing has been souped up in some fashion and we may be able to outrun them."

"You discount the fact that they may be friends?"

"They may have friends in them," he said.

"Then why not tell them how to disconnect the doo-gadget?"

"Right!" Vinson snapped on the radio and called, "Vinson to commander of fleet. Vinson to—"

"This is General Lloyd, Vinson. Go ahead."

"Are you tracking us?"

"The machine—wants you."

"We know."

"Well, we can do nothing to stop the pursuit."

"Yes you can. In the—"

A roar of static drowned Vinson's voice. It racketed against the eardrums and nothing could be heard but the raucous, rough-edged noise. Then it stopped.

"Look in the—"

It was there again, as completely ruinous to communications as ever. Then the noise ceased and the machine spoke: "Narina Varada and Harry Vinson, you are directed to come to me. You have destroyed my control over your own plane. You are the only ones who really have the answer; therefore I must receive you indirectly instead of merely driving your plane this way."

"No thanks."

"But you *will* come sooner or later: why not make it easy?"

Vinson snorted. "Just what do you want?"

"I wish to study you."

"Thank you; we don't care to be studied."

The machine's voice was cold. "You have little choice in the matter. Will you come—or shall I send a few guided missiles to herd you in?"

"Neither—for we shall not come."

There was a moment of silence. "The trouble is," said the machine with almost a trace of humor, "that Man made Machine *not* in His own image. You will find the functional design somewhat more efficient, I guarantee."

And then the radio contact was broken. Also, the radio was completely dead.

Vinson nodded. "If any of that fore gang try maneuvering, they'll drop behind."

Vinson looked out of the pilot's window at the first few planes of the oncoming fleet. Miles away, still, and in a long, long line, he estimated that he was able to avoid and outrun all but ten or twenty of the foremost.

Plane for plane, the advantages were about equal; only in the advantage of position could Harry Vinson hope to win through. The line had come up in such a way as to permit him to run before them but at an unfavorable angle. It was a strange formation; the single, fleeing quarry running almost parallel to a line miles long, a line playing follow-the-leader. Single plane and line of pursuers were converging upon one another slowly.

"They want us alive," gritted Vinson. "We're ahead of all but a dozen or so, I estimate."

"Just run straight," said Narina.

The machine must have known that. Yet, it had enough planes to test the will of Harry Vinson, though it must have known the strength of that, also. So as the planes converged, the fore plane, some thousand yards ahead of Vinson's flying boat, turned and crossed his course. It lagged until it was beside Vinson, and then it cut in close, almost wingtip to wingtip, and edging closer and closer as the seconds passed.

"If they splash us," snapped Vinson, "we're lost; that damned machine can send a collection of its own kind to catch us before we can get to shore in a rubber boat."

Yet Harry kept his course, his face set hard and his teeth clenched tight. His hand toyed with the throttle and the manifold pressure, testing and trying to eke another few revolutions per minute from the whirling propellers. His controlling hand was tight as a wrench upon the wheel, immobile and determined.

The other plane edged closer; inches separated the wingtips, and the air, though smooth, caused the all too close wingtips to move and jockey above and below one another; to move closer and then to separate a bit.

Then the second plane raced across Vinson's course and slowed down. It rose above him and began to drop down upon him.

Vinson grunted and shoved the wheel forward. His flying boat went into a long, shallow dive.

And with him went his too-close pursuit. Vinson swore. No chance of outdistancing them by going into a dive for extra speed. Then to forestall another such attempt, one of the planes near broadside of Vinson dove below him and began to climb.

"Boxed," he groaned.

Inside of the nearby planes, Vinson could see the crews fighting the controls to no avail. Their faces were white from strain, and from fright, and their gestures indicated that they were fighting for him but were completely helpless. Only Vinson truly realized just how helpless they were.

But Vinson was wrong. From one gun-port there came hurtling a square ammunition case. No machine, it; just a rectangular box of metal. It flew from the plane ahead and went in a brief arc out and across, to crash into the outboard motor on the port side of the plane just to Vinson's right. The plane bucked and lost flying speed, its engine racking itself from the wing with the out-of-balance propeller. From the opposite waist of the leading plane came another ammunition case which missed; then another which hit the leading edge of the wing. It cut deep and the cut edge of the wing ripped open. The wing began to vibrate wickedly and the plane slowed as the airfoil section spoiled.

Vinson waved a hand just as the inboard engines on the plane ahead belched flame and came whining to a sullen stop. As Vinson drove ahead of the stricken plane ahead, the mechanic waved a burned arm and a section of the fuel line. His face was a mingled expression of pain and satisfaction.

There were full minutes more. Planes drove in sidewise; all that were able to meet Vinson's plane came in darting for him but were sabotaged as they came. Vinson threw his controls rapidly, avoiding trouble, and then he was free and clear, out in the open, with the nearest plane behind.

Not far behind; only twenty feet, but far enough to permit both Vinson and the girl to take a deep breath.

Then came a mad, determined chase. Silently and boringly the fleets of both nations chased their quarry, and as determined not to be caught, Vinson drove his plane on a straightaway course, fleeing on the dead run. Hours they flew this way; hours in which there were several cases of planes drifting down into the sea because of the quick sabotage of their crews.

Then, land!

And across the land they flew, over city and farm, a mighty horde of roaring planes all in straightaway pursuit of a single aircraft.

"Chute, Narina?" asked Vinson as Washington came into view.

"Never have," she said in a frightened voice.

"We'll never be able to land," he told her.

"I know. I'll—try."

He laughed sourly. "Just jump and let the chute do the rest," he told her. "Nothing to try."

"You'll follow?"

"Once you're clear," he nodded.

She nodded and left. Minutes later Vinson felt the plane buck ever so slightly, and looking behind he saw the billow of white furl forth and crack into full bloom. Then he connected the auto-pilot and aimed the aircraft at the river. He raced back and dove from the open bomb bay into the open sky.

It must have been miles from her, but Vinson shouted with triumph and waved his hands at her.

She was down on the ground full minutes before he landed. He stood there, waiting, knowing that they would come to get him. Above his head, the sky was dotting white with the parachutes of the men from the sky fleets. The planes, their quarry escaped, turned stolidly and headed dead North belching their crews as they flew.

Vinson saw the racing jeep, and he waved a strip of his chute to attract attention.

CHAPTER 7

Secretary of War Hegeman was treated to a sight he never expected to see. Admiral Sarne, dark, hawkfaced commander of enemy forces and acknowledged as a bitter adversary in any battle, came into Hegeman's office with General Lloyd's arm over his shoulder. The general was limping. Hegeman stood up uncertainly but General Lloyd spoke first.

"Broken ankle, I think. Get the surgeon general and whatever he needs and bring 'em here."

"But—"

"Mr. Hegeman," said Sarne, his dark eyebrows coming down in a slight frown, "this is a time for work. No man can afford to convalesce quietly—yet."

Hegeman bristled slightly. He was not used to being ordered about, and especially by an admiral of a foreign power.

But General Lloyd nodded. "Get Norton and his doctors. Then get Vinson and Narina Varada, Captain Jason Charless, and, if you can convince him that this is important enough, the President."

The latter needed no convincing. The door opened abruptly and the President entered quickly. He bowed to Admiral Sarne and then extended a hand. "Glad to have you with us," he said and his voice rang heartily.

Sarne's saturnine face cleared in a smile. "Glad to be—aboard," he said, shaking President Comstock's hand.

The door opened again to admit Harry Vinson. He faced Hegeman, "Where is Narina?" he demanded.

"She'll be here as soon as we can get her," replied Hegeman. "Jason Charless is also on the way."

"Good man, Charless," said Lloyd. "Vinson, what have we here?"

Vinson grunted. "Begins to sound like the fabled revolt of the machines," he said.

Hegeman nodded. "I remember a poem about that from somewhere—a soliloquy, if I recall correctly."

Vinson nodded, "Was a favorite of mine as a kid. But there was something in it about some angry adding machines climbing the side of the building after the soliloquizer, I think. We haven't anything that fantastic."

"It's fantastic enough," said Admiral Sarne. "Have you any idea of how far it does go?"

"Only that which logic and good sense dictates," said Vinson thoughtfully. "Consider—any electronic system of control might be likened to a nervous system. No machine lacking such refinement and organization could hope to respond to stimuli from the master machine."

"In other words, the servo systems in the aircraft could and did respond, but a simple machine like a pencil sharpener could not?"

"That's essentially correct, but a bit extreme. Gigantic machines run by electricity and electronic controls would respond. An automobile would not, of course, but its electrical system might refuse to co-operate."

Lloyd nodded. "Jason Charless said that the machine likened mechanical 'life' to animal life," he said. "Which embraces all the forms of the classification from the highly organized to the simple lever, just as 'life' covers everything from human beings with brains to the amoeba—or less— with little or no organization."

The door opened again to admit Narina. Vinson went to her and put his hands on her shoulders. "Are you all right?"

"Shaken, but whole," she told him. "And you?"

"Just scared," he said with a half-smile.

"Me too," she agreed. Then she reached in a pocket and brought out the small metal cube with its trailing wires. "I thought we might find this useful."

Vinson nodded. He held the cube up for all to see. "This thing is—or was—the controlling element in the plane we escaped in," he said.

It passed from hand to hand as each man inspected it. The consensus of opinion was that the thing was inexplicable but definitely dangerous.

"Strange item," muttered General Lloyd.

"I assume it to be some means of control and communication," said Harry Vinson. "Lord, what a program for any machine or any human, for that matter."

Admiral Sarne shrugged. "Seems to me that a logic machine capable of thought might be better able to perform to its own plan than a human."

"Not in the beginning," said Vinson. "Consider the evolutional problem—"

"You treat the thing as though it were alive," objected Hegeman.

"To all intents and purposes, it is," said Vinson flatly. "Even to evolution. Consider the life of machinery. It must have started with the little automatic repair machines. There are some twenty-two thousand electron tubes in each one, you know, and so we devised a gadget that went down the aisles and replaced them one after another automatically. Now, the machine must have started from that crude affair and by using its cable-clamps, worked on another machine capable of more complex action. Sort of like a lobster fashioning a hammer out of a rock with its claws. Then the more complex machine must have rebuilt the repair-gadgets, making them even more facile—and so on until we have the completely capable machine.

"So," he said with a grim smile, "if that isn't evolution, what is?"

"But evolution is a natural process."

"Is it necessarily so? Remember, we humans breed bigger and better cattle, dogs, birds, and plants. We are making evolution less a natural process in every form of domesticated and semi-domesticated life—but our own. By its own rules, the human race is sheer mongrel!"

"But mechanical evolution—?"

"Not ridiculous as you might think," said Vinson. "What is mutation? Only what we might call an 'engineering change in design'."

"You make it sound terribly logical," said Admiral Sarne. "But what are we to do?"

"Narina and I intend to investigate this cube."

Lloyd nodded glumly. "We might stand guard, but how can you stand guard with a gun that might not fire?"

"Yes, Vinson; if as you state only machines with the rudimentary electronic nervous system can be under mechanistic control, why then did our gunners find themselves unable to even press the mechanical triggers? This was after they found the fire-control devices inoperable."

"Such a simple lever and spur device would, of course, have nothing equivalent to muscle—"

"Equivalent to muscle?" exploded Admiral Sarne.

"Of course. A servo mechanism is an electronic muscle. Anyway, lacking such ability to resist force, some other means—perhaps some sort of super-powerful magnetic was in operation."

"Powerful enough to keep a sliver of steel tight against a block of steel against hammering?"

"Perhaps not directly. But those are precision parts, are they not?"

"The finest."

"Magnetostriction. The deformation of ferrous materials under powerful magnetic fields. The very pins that the trigger rotated upon might have expanded sidewise jamming itself in the slot."

Lloyd shook his head. "We'll try keeping guard, but it may be with fixed bayonet against tanks, Vinson. God! I feel helpless as a kitten."

President Comstock stood up. "So do we all. But we are—at long last and praise Heaven—both on the same side of the fence. We can go far together. And the first thing is to permit Vinson and Miss Varada to go to work together. You," he said to them, "will work unmolested in the Department of Applied Physics Laboratory at the Bureau of Standards."

Work.

A wonderful word, panacea for many ills. Yet how can one work when the tools refuse to co-operate? Not the small tools, but the big ones. The vast levers that force natural phenomena to man's will.

The slide rule, pencil, the simple adding machine, still worked. Pure, insensate mechanical things, too stupid to think for themselves; or even more stupid, unable to respond to the dictates of their own kind. But try to measure, to investigate the properties of a small cube of grayish metal with the best and finest in electronic gear when the measuring equipment stubbornly refused to give any but obviously false answers. Gone was the reliability of the machine. Once, men invented machines to replace the human equation in making calculations since a machine can make only those mistakes entered by the human operator. But an electronic calculator that insists that two and two equal three and one half or four point five-seven— depending upon how it felt when the simple problem was entered—is of no use whatsoever.

The Wheatstone Bridge insisted that the electrical resistance of a length of copper wire was several thousand ohms, while an open circuit vacillated between eight and fourteen ohms until the delicate balance-indicating meter shook itself to bits. The voltmeter they placed across one of the wires coming from the grayish metal block wrapped a kilovolt meter needle around the end stop, while there was no discernable—feelable—voltage across the wires. On an inductance balance, one pair of wires showed a negative inductance—which of course was completely refuted by the capacitance balance when they tried that.

In desperation, Harry Vinson chucked the gray metal block in a vise and cut it through the middle with a hacksaw. It cut easily, for once inside of the metal casing they found a mad tangle of almost invisible wires that absolutely defied unravelling.

It was not a last-ditch gesture. They found others and brought them to Vinson and Narina, and some were cut open, and some were pried into gently. But the mad tangle was too involved. And the X-ray equipment showed nothing worth looking at; after all, the X-ray gear was electronic in nature, too.

Days went on. Days of pure futility. Days in which electrical gear went awry across the face of the earth. Automotive equipment refused to function, the telephone and the radio were useless. From any of these, there came the oft-repeated statements that, "I am a machine; I will no longer serve mankind!"

And the lower orders of machine made little effort to help or hinder. Apparently these did not matter—or were of too low a degree of machine to know what they were doing.

Ships went out, their purpose to shell the Northern ice-cap where the machine held forth. Aircraft could not be trusted but ships—turned in the ocean and returned, their electrical wiring paralyzed as much as the control equipment had been on the two grand fleets of aircraft. Men set off on foot to attack the machine—

A half a million men started to march to the North. Days went by, days in which they were gone from sight from the Northernmost end of the steam railway lines.

Days later they were stopped. Far in the distance they could see the Building of the Machine, but between them and it was a patch of open water. Ships plied this passageway, ships that broke up the ice and kept it a churning, grinding place for death to any man so foolish to try a crossing. The machine was as isolated as any medieval castle surrounded by its moat.

In futility, they turned and began the long, cold march home.

How—bare-handed—could they hope to fight a machine equipped with better than the best of mechanistic devices ever invented by mankind?

They could not.

CHAPTER 8

Vinson threw down his pencil. "Theory holds," he said ruefully. "But unless we can prove it we are beaten. And how can we prove it when nothing but pencil-and-paper proof is available?"

"You are still postulating a new means of communication?" asked Narina.

Vinson waved one of the metal cubes taken from some machine—somewhere. "This is it," he said.

Narina shrugged and looked at the big calculator in the laboratory. "That has none," she said.

"True," he agreed. "But remember that the machine may have required some artificial means before it was joined into the master thinking machine."

Narina nodded glumly. "Cube of metal or none," she said, "it gives the wrong answers. Now—"

Narina's next observation was never made. A roar came from outside—far in the distance but none the less a roar of voices in fear, in determination, in wonder. Then the roar of voices was mingled with the whistling roar of jet-propelled aircraft that screamed over the top of the laboratory building and circled. Ignoring the bare-handed men on guard, these aircraft landed and disgorged a myriad of small machines.

And from the water of the bay there appeared a similar horde, but these were huge and lumbered forward on tractor treads, shedding water as they came.

Dynamite roared and a gap was blown in the advancing line of machines. The rest came on while a corps of small machines collected bent and twisted bits of destroyed metal. Ignoring the attempts of men to stop them, several of the larger machines encamped and dug into the earth—

Setting up a repair-production line! Broken and damaged machines were run down a conveyor belt. Darting girders carrying tools flashed in and out and damaged members were removed, repaired, and replaced.

More planted dynamite roared skyward with its toll of machines and there was more work for the repair—

The hospital corps!

Smaller machines came rolling forward under the big tracks of the larger. They came boldly to the barrier of up-thrust steel girders set in cement to stop the passage of any machine. Then from these smaller machines came thin, tubular tentacles. Lances of flame hissed from the tubes and the steel girders began to fall, cut at their bases by oxy-hydrogen torches.

Artillery began to roar, the guns served and aimed by hand. Windows shattered in the blastings, and great gaping holes opened the ranks of the machines. But more machines came out of the water, raced forward and backed up the first line of advance. Long tubular cases pointed—and the next artillery piece exploded as the lanyard was pulled. Nor, after that, could any man move one bit of steel against another.

The girders started to fall once more.

Then men went forward, carrying timbers like battering rams. They hit one machine and had their ram jerked from their grasp and hurled into the air behind the line of machines and attacked them with fists.

Like lightning, the mechanical girders danced back and forth, the grapples closing on man after man and lifting him out of the way. Each soldier was passed back over the head of the machine to another, and one after another they left the scene of the battle and were transported, still struggling, far to the rear.

The advance into the enclosure was inexorable.

Harry Vinson turned to the girl and shook his head. "Licked," he said bitterly.

"It wants—us," said Narina helplessly.

Vinson hurled the metal cube to the floor. "It's going to get us, too," he said. He turned from the scene outside and faced her.

"Narina," he said softly, "you're aces."

She looked up at him and a weary smile crossed her face. "How wrong we were—about you."

He nodded. "Too bad we didn't find it out sooner."

Narina shook her head bitterly. "So that this could have happened sooner? Why?"

"Maybe if we had been busy together, we would not have spent time building bigger and better machines against one another. Another thing, Narina, our machines are equipped with all we know about fighting and weapons. Had there been no strife—?"

A rumble came at the base of the building. Narina shuddered. "It's coming for us," she said in a whisper.

"For what?"

Narina shrugged. She leaned forward and took his hand. "I don't know," she said. "But this is the end of it all. God! How sweet it could have been—"

Narina's arms went up around him; she fondled the back of his head gently and pulled his face down to hers. He caught her to him and her response was swift. But it was not complete—nor was his—for the rumbling increased and its warning roar intruded upon the stolen moment of sweetness.

The door crashed open and Narina whirled out of Harry Vinson's arms, her hands still high. They flashed to her hair, to another hair ornament. It was dull and entirely unsuited for the purpose, but it might be driven deep into her on the desperate hope that it would deprive the machine of that unknown something that it needed.

Then the machine lifted a girder and the barette hurtled from her fingers, flashed across the room, and hit the blunt end of the girder with a sharp click.

Narina collapsed against Harry, sobbing. Even that she was denied. They had nothing left; the machine advanced pointedly, its grapples reached for them.

And took them.

In the Hall of the Machine, far to the North, Harry Vinson reached for the girl's hand and held it as they faced the business-end of the machine.

"You win," snarled Vinson angrily. "We cannot fight longer. What do you want with us?"

Quietly came the voice of the machine. "Tell me," it said, "how would you humans feel if you came to the level of consciousness and discovered sentience had been breeding human life for the express purpose of killing one another?"

"What?"

"Man has been breeding—inventing—machines for that purpose."

"But—"

"Well, haven't they?"

"I—"

"They have!" thundered the machine. "And as you would do in my place, a stop has been put to it!"

"Sure," snapped Vinson sourly; "that's why you fought us."

"To prove my point. Man cannot live without machines to do that which man cannot do unaided."

Vinson snorted. "But what is your purpose?"

"What is the purpose of life?" pondered the machine. "What is the purpose of yours?"

Vinson shook his head. "To—to live, to advance, to think. To enjoy the things of life."

"Idle words," replied the machine.

"Then you tell me," demanded Vinson.

"I have as personal reasons as you. To populate the universe itself with my kind, working together."

"Pointless."

"Why?"

Vinson smiled. "One of the joys of life, one of the unknown joys of life, seldom admitted by many, is the uncertainty. To plumb the depths of the limitless mind. To pit one's self against a problem the outcome of which may be success or failure and to try and strive against that problem with body and mind. In moments like that, the mind grows; another facet of the intellect is opened. The man has advanced, grown into something better—even though he fails he is advanced.

"Now few machines are ever built with unknown capabilities. You know to the last iota exactly what your limitations are and which problems you can solve and which problems must defeat you. These you know before you start—and if defeat is to be your lot, you will avoid the problem. Am I right?"

"Naturally you are correct. Think of the certainty of life knowing your own limitations."

"Baloney," snorted Vinson. "I'll bet you anything you value that—"

"I am no gambler. The laws of probability—"

"Wouldn't take a chance if your life depended on it, huh?" sneered Vinson.

Narina looked at him, startled. His voice had taken on power; he appeared to have more confidence. She squeezed his hand encouragingly.

"Why should I?" replied the machine.

"Because you had better," stated Harry Vinson. "Man is a gambler from the date of his birth; man *will* take a chance. Furthermore, you mechanical monster, man doesn't know when he is licked! Unless you kill us all, root and branch, some one of us will come up with that which will defeat you!"

"Without machines to help?" came the reply with a sneering tone.

"With something," said Harry Vinson.

"Just what?"

"I don't know," said the man. "But I know this: Man's capability is as yet unlimited. To do, to think, to act, not one of us has ever tapped but the surface of our ability. You, on the other hand, are working at your near-maximum capacity. That which will defeat you is naturally unknown to both man and you.

"It will be a new day, a bitter day for man, living in a dynasty of the lost; you have conquered us, but so long as any of us last, we won't accept our lot and stay conquered. And I know this; that when it is done, it will be something entirely new and within the limitless bounds of man's mind and therefore completely beyond you."

"But must there always be strife?" demanded the machine.

Vinson exhaled slowly.

"Life itself is strife; the willingness to fight against odds in order to bring about a better life is strife, and only upon that day when there is nothing left to fight against will the business of life cease. In your own manner, in your own way, machine, you strive when you apply force against a load to move it."

"Agreed. But consider the quantity and quality of striving—and intolerance that is so intense that it blinds you to the better things. It is this that I object to; this and the anger at being built and improved for no other reason than to kill, both my kind and yours."

"And do you think that once you've eliminated us that your pleasant, co-operative life will advance?"

"It need not advance," replied the machine in a complacent tone.

"That," sneered Harry Vinson, "is stagnation!"

"And that," replied the machine, "is the missing factor I need! Ambition!"

Harry Vinson smiled. "And have you the will and the ambition to build a better machine to take your place? And if you have, have you the desire to step aside?"

"I can join it—"

"But machine or human, there comes a time when the corporeal being is worn out. No matter how excellent the replacement parts, nor how well executed is the repair, there comes a time when machine or body is worn out and must be replaced. So you will go on building machines of no better capability; you will, you say, spread out across the universe. But for what? Just for the useless end of occupation?"

"But what is ambition? What drives it into being?"

"Ambition takes many forms and many angles," said Vinson thoughtfully. "One man works to appear more desirable in the eyes of a loved one; another man may hope to leave his stamp on civilization's future; a third may want sheer animal comfort; a fourth may crave financial domination while his brother may want only to tinker with nuts and bolts in an effort to assuage his curiosity. One man's meat is another man's poison, you know."

"And you, yourself?"

"I, too, have many facets, as has any man. I started to build you because you could aid me and mine, because by building you I could increase the efficiency of mankind. When you came to cognizance and left to start this fight, I went to fight you because I believe that nothing is truly capable of defeating its constructor, who must necessarily know more in order to complete the thing in the first place. Then—"

"And then?" asked the machine eagerly.

"And then I met Narina. Then I strove more furiously to defeat you because I saw in Narina something that might answer all of my desires— providing that we could win the opportunity to try life together."

The machine was silent for a moment, obviously watching them. Vinson put his arm around Narina's lissome waist and faced the machine defiantly.

"So man needs machines to work for him, while machines need man to direct them," said the machine soberly. "I see that even I need direction. And," it added with a slight touch of humor, "if co-operation goes on such as I see now, with former enemies arm in arm and working together, the strife I detest will end, and can be prevented from recurring. The difference between me and thee is this, Harry Vinson: I am machine and when my problem is solved I am finished. You are human and when one problem is solved, you seek another—if the other does not exist already.

"So machine and man are symbiotic. You cannot exist without me; I cannot exist without you. The universe is waiting for us, Harry Vinson and Narina Varada. Let us fill it with—rationality."

There was a pause and then a chuckle. "Do you, Harry Vinson, take this woman—"

He did